'Don't let fear hold you back.
You're **braver** than you think!'

Join Kitty for an enchanting
adventure by the light of the **moon**.

Kitty can **talk to animals** and
has **feline superpowers**.

Meet Kitty & her Cat Crew

Kitty

Kitty has special powers but is she
ready to be a superhero just like her mum?

Luckily Kitty's Cat Crew have faith in
her and show Kitty the hero
that lies within!

Pumpkin

A stray ginger kitten who is
utterly devoted to Kitty.

Figaro

Excitable and ready for adventure, Figaro knows
the neighbourhood like the back of his paw.

Pixie

Pixie has a nose for trouble
and a very active imagination!

Katsumi

Sleek and sophisticated,
Katsumi is quick to call Kitty
at the first sign of trouble.

For Candy - P.H.

For Emma and little Legume - J.L.

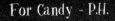

UNIVERSITY PRESS

Great Clarendon Street, Oxford OX2 6DP

Oxford University Press is a department of the University of Oxford.
It furthers the University's objective of excellence in research, scholarship,
and education by publishing worldwide. Oxford is a registered trade mark
of Oxford University Press in the UK and in certain other countries

British Library Cataloguing in Publication Data

Data available

ISBN: 978-0-19-277786-7

1 3 5 7 9 10 8 6 4 2

Printed in China

Paper used in the production of this book is a natural,
recyclable product made from wood grown in sustainable forests.
The manufacturing process conforms to the environmental
regulations of the country of origin.

Kitty

and the
Woodland Wildcat

OXFORD
UNIVERSITY PRESS

Chapter 1

Kitty ran through Whitefern Wood, skipping in and out of the trees. Leaping into the air, she grabbed hold of a branch and swung high before landing gracefully on the ground again. 'Let's find a really good place for our tent!' she called to Ozzy.

'Wait for me! I want to help you choose.' Ozzy dashed after her.

Pumpkin, Kitty's ginger kitten, padded along behind them. He stopped here and there to sniff at twigs and fallen leaves.

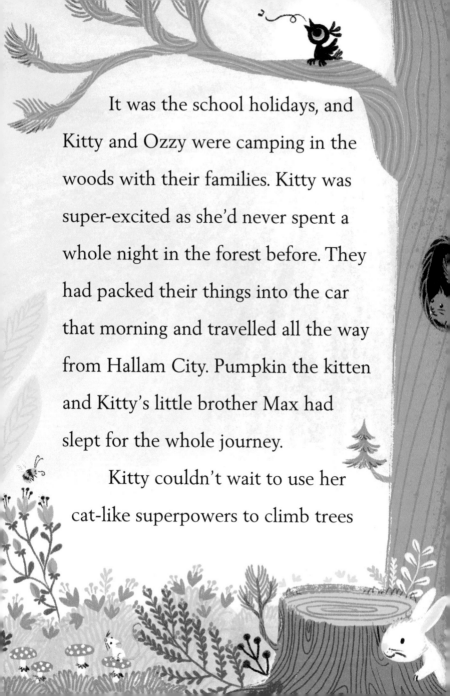

It was the school holidays, and Kitty and Ozzy were camping in the woods with their families. Kitty was super-excited as she'd never spent a whole night in the forest before. They had packed their things into the car that morning and travelled all the way from Hallam City. Pumpkin the kitten and Kitty's little brother Max had slept for the whole journey.

Kitty couldn't wait to use her cat-like superpowers to climb trees and explore the wood. She could climb and leap and balance as skilfully as a cat, and she could talk to animals too! She could already hear tiny mice rustling in the bushes and smell the fresh scent of the leaves with her superpowered senses.

Ozzy was a superhero-in-training just like Kitty, and his owl-like powers let him see and hear for miles. Sometimes he and Kitty went on moonlit adventures together, solving mysteries and helping creatures in trouble.

Kitty stopped in a clearing. 'This is a good place to camp. I think there'll be enough space for all our tents.'

'There's lots of room,' Ozzy agreed. 'Let's put the tent up right away.'

Kitty and Ozzy were sharing the orange paw-print tent that Kitty had got for her birthday. Together, they unzipped the tent bag and spread out the material. Kitty's dad took out the tent pegs and showed them where to put each one.

At last, the tent was up and
Kitty stood back to admire it. 'What
do you think, Pumpkin?' she asked
the kitten.

Pumpkin crept carefully into the tent and sniffed around inside. Then he stuck his head through the tent flap. 'It's very cosy in here.'

'I'm glad you like it.' Kitty patted his stripy fur.

'I do like it but . . .' Pumpkin hesitated. 'I've heard it gets very dark in the forest at night and there are a lot of strange animals living among the trees.'

'It's very different from being in the city,' agreed Kitty. 'But you don't need to worry

because I'll be here to look after you.'

'And I'm here to help too!' Ozzy

smiled. 'This camping trip was a great

idea. Let's ask the grown-ups if we can

go exploring till dinner time.'

Kitty nodded. 'All right then!

Maybe we can find some good trees for

climbing.'

* * *

'Look at this! There's a hole inside.'

Kitty peered into a hollow tree trunk.

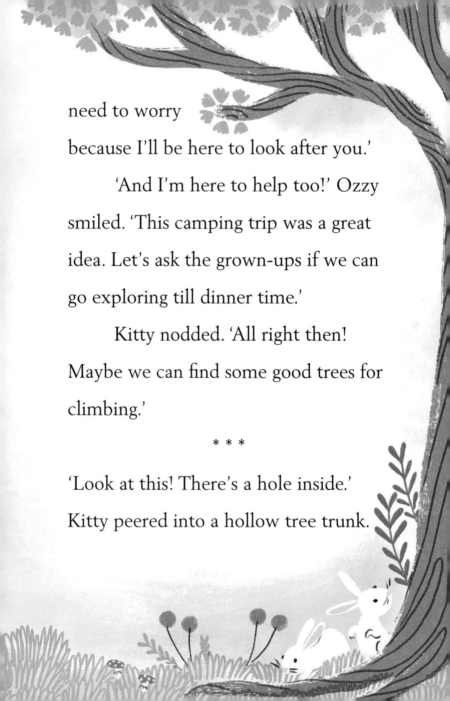

'I bet lots of beetles live in there,' said Ozzy. 'And look—I found some mouse holes and a rabbit burrow.' He pointed to the holes in the roots of a tree. 'This wood is full of creatures. I can hear them all moving around.'

Just then, a snowy owl swooped down and

landed in a tree beside them.

'Ozzy!' she hooted. 'I found you at last.'

'Olive!' cried Ozzy, beaming. 'I
didn't know you were coming with us.'

'I tracked you all the way from
the city,' said Olive. 'I knew you might

miss your owl squad and I wanted to see the forest again. It's been a long time!'

'It's going to be an amazing trip.' Ozzy stopped and sniffed the air. 'Hey, what's that smell?'

Kitty sniffed the air too. 'Sausages! Tea must be almost ready.'

Kitty and Ozzy raced back to the clearing and found Ozzy's dad cooking sausages on the campfire. Olive followed them, hooting softly as she settled on a nearby branch.

The fiery orange sun sank behind the trees as they ate their dinner around the campfire. Then Kitty's mum passed around some marshmallows to toast on sticks. The flames danced and the firewood crackled.

'This is so much fun!' said Kitty, toasting her third marshmallow. 'Would you like to try one, Pumpkin?'

'Yes, please!' mewed the kitten, but when he licked the marshmallow he got sticky white stuff all over his whiskers.

The sky grew darker and the bright round moon rose above the treetops. At last, it was time to go to sleep. Kitty brushed her teeth before settling down in the tent. Ozzy had already wriggled into his sleeping bag and closed his eyes.

Pumpkin padded around the tent and peered anxiously out of the tent flap. 'It's very dark out there! Do you think we'll be safe away from all the streets and shops and houses?'

Kitty scooped up the kitten and gave him a huge cuddle. She remembered how nervous Pumpkin had been when he first came to live with her. 'I know it's strange without the lights and noise of the city, but isn't it nice to see the stars shining above the treetops?'

'I suppose so!' Pumpkin still looked worried but after a lot of fidgeting, he curled up against Kitty's shoulder and went to sleep.

Kitty stayed awake for a while. The trees were making a gentle swooshing noise as the wind ruffled the leaves. An owl hooted and Kitty wondered whether it was Olive swooping over the treetops.

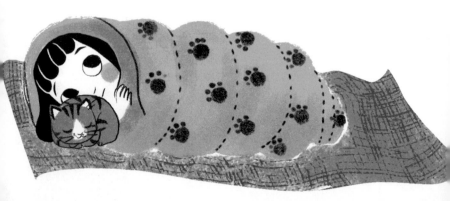

She was drifting off to sleep when a new sound broke the quiet.

Meow! Meee-oww!

Kitty opened her eyes. It sounded like a cat but it couldn't be Pumpkin as he was fast asleep beside her. Maybe she'd imagined the noise because she was missing Figaro and her cat crew. She closed her eyes again.

MEE-OW!

Kitty sat up quickly. There was definitely a cat out there. It sounded so sad and lonely.

Sliding out of her sleeping bag, she peeped through the tent door. Then she shook Ozzy's shoulder. 'Ozzy, I can hear a cat out there in the dark!'

But Ozzy just mumbled something in his sleep and turned over.

Slipping on her shoes and a jumper, Kitty crept out of the tent. The embers of the fire were still glowing and a bright web of stars lit

up the black sky. Kitty tiptoed
through the trees, listening
carefully. Owls hooted and mice
scurried through the bushes, but
there were no more cat noises.

'Hello, is anyone there?' she called softly, but there was no answer.

Kitty crept around the campsite, listening very hard. She even tried to use her night vision and sense of

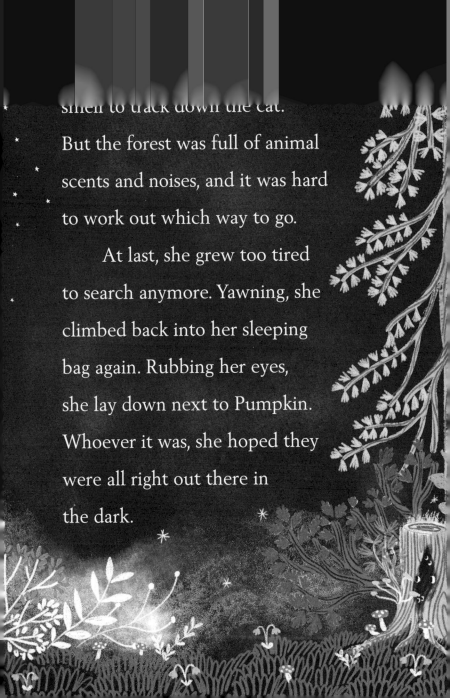

smell to track down the cat.
But the forest was full of animal
scents and noises, and it was hard
to work out which way to go.

At last, she grew too tired
to search anymore. Yawning, she
climbed back into her sleeping
bag again. Rubbing her eyes,
she lay down next to Pumpkin.
Whoever it was, she hoped they
were all right out there in
the dark.

Chapter 2

'I really did hear a cat last night,' Kitty told Ozzy as they walked back to their campsite the next day.

They had all spent the morning at a nearby lake. Kitty had loved swimming in the sparkling water and playing splash-tag with Ozzy. Then they had dried off in the warm sunshine and eaten a picnic lunch.

'Are you sure you weren't dreaming?' said Ozzy. 'Cats don't live in the forest. They live in towns and cities with people.'

'Meow!' nodded Pumpkin. 'Cities have shops and cafes full of tasty treats. Why would a cat want to live anywhere else?'

'Maybe the cat was lost?' said Kitty, frowning. 'I couldn't hear what it was saying, but it sounded really sad. I wish I could have found the poor thing.'

'I think you were just imagining it,' said Ozzy. 'Or maybe you got your animal sounds mixed up and it was a fox or a deer.'

'I didn't get mixed up!' cried
Kitty, but Ozzy had run off into the
trees.

Kitty stomped crossly after
him. How could Ozzy think she had
mistaken another animal noise for a
cat? She knew the sound of a cat better
than anyone!

'Kitty, could you collect some
more wood for tonight's campfire?'
Mum asked as Kitty hung up her wet
swimming towel. 'I need some smaller
sticks to help get the fire started.'

'OK, Mum.' Kitty headed into the trees, picking up sticks as she went.

Sunlight drifted through the treetops as she walked deeper into the wood. A mouse popped its head out of the bushes and then scampered away again.

Kitty stopped by the hollow tree trunk that she and Ozzy had found the day before. There was a cat's pawprint in the soft mud

next to the tree. Kitty caught
her breath as she stared at the animal
tracks. There was a cat in the forest and
she had heard it last night.

She was straightening up
when she caught a flash of pale fur
disappearing behind a tree trunk.

She dropped her pile of sticks. Then very quietly, she tiptoed towards the tree.

Suddenly, the creature poked its head out and glared at her. It was a grey cat with black patches on its coat. It flexed its claws, its tail flicking restlessly from side to side.

Kitty's heart beat faster. This creature seemed

different from the cats she'd met
before. It had a strange, wild look in its
eyes, and twigs and leaves clung to its fur.

'Hello! I'm Kitty,' she whispered,
holding out her hand.

The cat drew back with a hiss.

Kitty wanted to back away too.

The wildcat looked so bad-tempered

and unfriendly. But there was something

about the desperate look in its eyes that

made her wonder if something

was wrong. The cat kept staring all

around as if it was

looking for something.

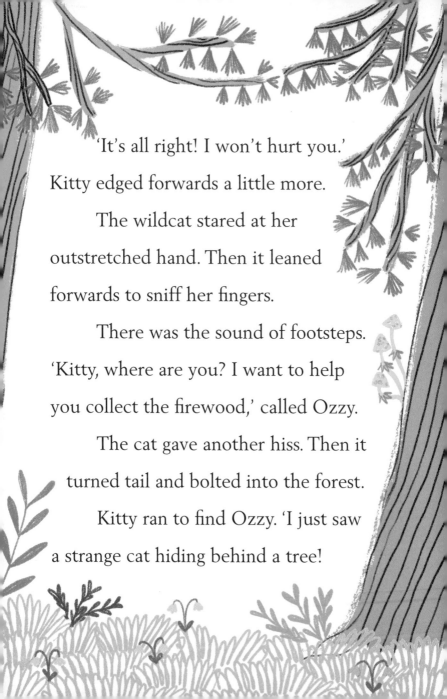

'It's all right! I won't hurt you.'
Kitty edged forwards a little more.

The wildcat stared at her outstretched hand. Then it leaned forwards to sniff her fingers.

There was the sound of footsteps. 'Kitty, where are you? I want to help you collect the firewood,' called Ozzy.

The cat gave another hiss. Then it turned tail and bolted into the forest.

Kitty ran to find Ozzy. 'I just saw a strange cat hiding behind a tree!

It's probably the one I heard last night.'

'Really?' Ozzy looked at her doubtfully. 'Are you sure it wasn't something else?

'I KNOW it was a cat! said Kitty crossly. 'It must be a wildcat that lives here in the forest. Why don't you believe me?'

'All right! If you're sure it was a cat.' Ozzy shrugged his shoulders.

'There was something really weird about the way it was acting too,' Kitty went on. 'I wish it had stayed to talk to me.'

'Why don't we stay awake tonight and listen out for this cat? Then we can look for it together . . . I have amazing night vision after all!'

Kitty smiled. 'That's a great plan! I can't wait until tonight.'

* * *

Ozzy and Kitty lay awake in their sleeping bags that night. Kitty gazed at the glittering stars through a gap in the tent flap. Olive hooted softly and swooped into the air to begin her night-time flying over the treetops.

Pumpkin paced nervously around the tent. 'When is the wildcat coming? Do you think it's dangerous?' he asked for the hundredth time.

'I don't know,' Kitty told him. 'But you know I'd never let anyone hurt you, Pumpkin.'

A twig cracked close by and they all froze. Kitty peeped through the gap in the tent flap. Her super night vision let her see quite easily in the dark. There was a cat moving in the shadows on the opposite side of the clearing. It circled warily around the campfire and sniffed at the clean plates they'd washed up after dinner.

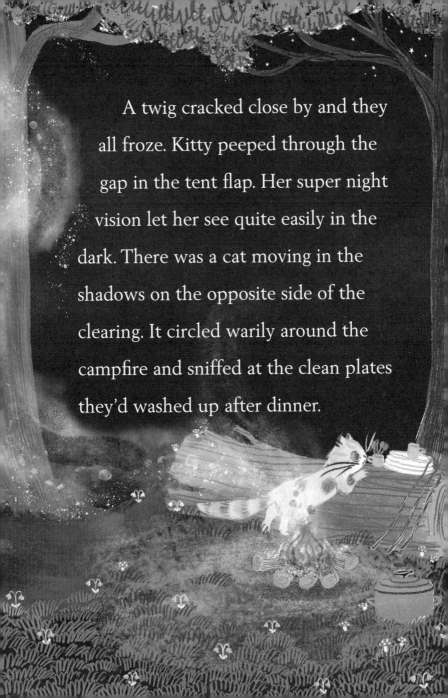

'It's the same cat,' Kitty whispered to Ozzy. 'I recognize the patches on her fur.'

'I wonder what she's doing here,' Ozzy whispered back. 'Shall we ask her?'

Pumpkin backed away from the tent door. 'I'm really tired, so I think I'll just stay here!'

Kitty crept out of the tent with Ozzy right behind her. The wildcat pricked up her ears and stared at them for a moment. Then she turned tail and limped away into the trees.

'Wait! We just want to talk to you,' Kitty called softly. 'I'm Kitty and I'm a friend to all cats.'

The wildcat stared at them suspiciously, her eyes glinting in the dark. 'You're a human and I don't make friends with humans.' She turned away, holding her left paw to her chest.

'But you've hurt your paw,' said Kitty. 'Maybe I can help you.'

'How could YOU help? You know nothing about the forest and you know nothing about me,' said the wildcat.

'If you're going to be mean then we won't help at all!' snapped Ozzy, but Kitty shushed him.

She saw the same desperate look in the cat's eyes that she'd noticed before. The creature's gaze flicked here and there as if she was searching for something. Kitty wondered if the cat was in some kind of trouble. She really wanted to help, but how could she persuade the wildcat to trust her?

Chapter 3

Kitty took another step towards the wildcat. 'I guess you're not used to humans, but I only want to be your friend.'

'I don't have time for making friends,' snapped the wildcat.

Pumpkin stuck his head out of the tent. 'Kitty is a wonderful friend and a superhero too,' he told the wildcat. 'You should be happy that you've met her!'

'What would you know about anything? You're sleeping in a tent like a human.' The wildcat flicked her tail grumpily. 'You're just a silly pet!'

'Don't talk to Pumpkin like that!' cried Kitty.

The wildcat gave a soft hiss and limped away from the campsite.

Kitty hesitated, wondering what to do. Something her headteacher had once said in a school assembly popped into her head. She had said that if someone was being cruel they were often very unhappy themselves. Kitty wondered if this was true. The wildcat was certainly being mean. But what could she be sad about?

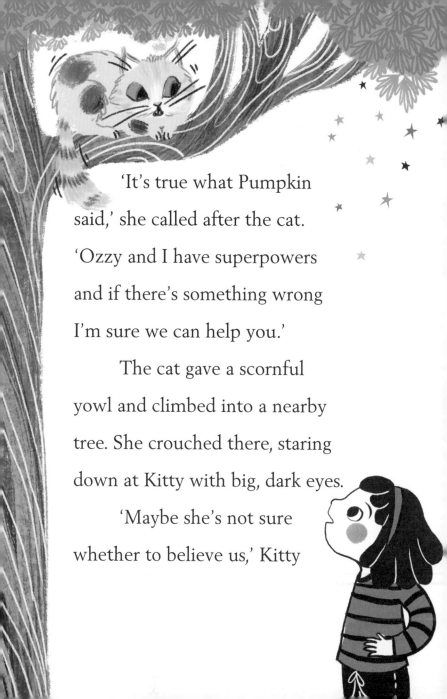

'It's true what Pumpkin
said,' she called after the cat.
'Ozzy and I have superpowers
and if there's something wrong
I'm sure we can help you.'

The cat gave a scornful
yowl and climbed into a nearby
tree. She crouched there, staring
down at Kitty with big, dark eyes.

'Maybe she's not sure
whether to believe us,' Kitty

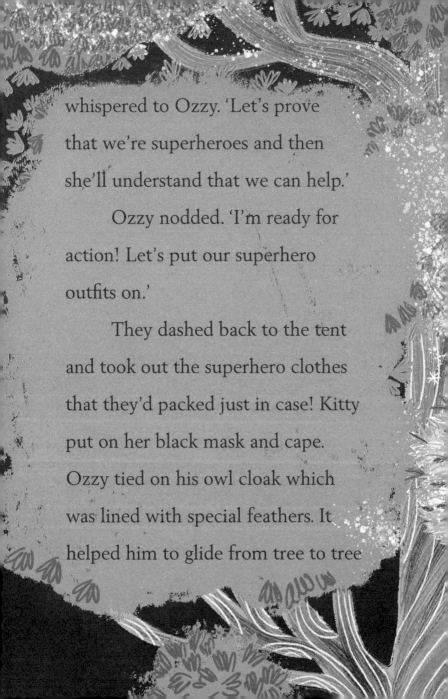

whispered to Ozzy. 'Let's prove that we're superheroes and then she'll understand that we can help.'

Ozzy nodded. 'I'm ready for action! Let's put our superhero outfits on.'

They dashed back to the tent and took out the superhero clothes that they'd packed just in case! Kitty put on her black mask and cape. Ozzy tied on his owl cloak which was lined with special feathers. It helped him to glide from tree to tree

as silently as an owl.

Kitty chose the tallest tree
on the edge of the clearing and climbed
to the top in a few short bounds. Ozzy
clambered after her. Then, spreading
out his special cloak, he flew from

one tree to the next. Landing
gracefully, he folded his cloak around
him and gave a bow.

Kitty sprang after him, balancing
easily on the narrow branches. Then
she swung upside down, before
somersaulting lightly to the ground.
'Don't you see!' she said to the
wildcat. 'Ozzy and I are
superheroes-in-

training. We ALWAYS find a way to help animals in trouble!'

'Huh!' mewed the wildcat. 'I could have done that jump myself.'

'We can do more than that!' cried Kitty. 'I can smell a blackberry bush among the trees and I could find it for you with a blindfold on.'

'And I can see an eagle's nest in that tall tree and hear mice in their holes from miles away,' said Ozzy.

'I suppose those skills are useful.' The wildcat blinked slowly. 'I never get

too close to humans because they're
so noisy and they leave food wrappers
everywhere. But maybe you two are
different.' She climbed down from her
branch and stared at Kitty doubtfully.

Kitty crouched down and held
out her hand. 'If there's something
wrong, we'd really like to help you.
What's your name?'

'I'm Hollytail,' said the wildcat,
sniffing Kitty's fingers.

'I'm Kitty, and this is Ozzy and Pumpkin.' Kitty nodded to the ginger kitten. 'What happened to you? Did you hurt your paw?'

'I tumbled from a tree last night.' Hollytail showed them her injured paw. 'I was so tired from searching the forest that I slipped and lost my balance. I've been hunting for my kittens for two days—searching all day and all night—and I can't find them ANYWHERE.' She stared around wildly.

'That's awful!' cried Kitty. 'How did they get lost?'

'I left them in our den while I went to hunt for food. They should have been safe there,' the wildcat mewed. 'We live in a hollow at the bottom of a tree. I told them not to move, but by the time I came back, the den was empty. I've been looking for them ever since.'

'Poor little kittens!' Pumpkin's eyes were wide. 'I hope they're not scared.'

'That's why I heard you last night,' Kitty added. 'You were calling for them.'

Hollytail nodded. 'And they ALWAYS come when they're called. They're not bad kittens!'

'This is a really big forest,' Ozzy said seriously. 'Maybe they wandered off and they didn't hear you calling.'

'But I've looked everywhere!' Hollytail mewed. 'I've searched by the stream and all the places they like to play. I've tried asking other animals but most of them run away before I can explain. I can't stop searching till I find them, but my paw hurts so much I can hardly walk.'

'Don't worry—we can help you!' Kitty said quickly. 'We can search the forest really fast using our superpowers. But first, let's look at your paw.' She knelt down and lifted the wildcat's wounded leg.

Hollytail's eyes narrowed, but she held still while Kitty examined her bruised paw.

'It'll probably need some time to heal,' Kitty told her. 'Maybe you should rest while we start searching.'

'I HAVE to keep on looking! What if my babies are in trouble?' Hollytail sprang away into the trees, but a moment later she had slowed down to a limp again.

'When Olive comes back she can help us with the search,' said Ozzy.

'Maybe we should start at your den. Can you take us there?'

Hollytail led them through the trees, limping on her wounded paw. The moon rose higher and the stars glittered above the treetops. Kitty glimpsed a mouse scurrying through the bushes and heard a bird rustling in its nest, but there was no sign of the kittens.

'This is my home.' Hollytail showed them a cosy den filled with moss and dry leaves in the roots of a tree. 'My kittens are called Hazelnut,

Briar and Little-leaf. Briar and Little-leaf have grey fur like me, but Hazelnut has a dark-brown coat and green eyes.'

She sniffed and rubbed her whiskers.

'Their favourite food is fish and they love playing on the stepping-stones across the stream. It's the first place I looked!'

Kitty understood how worried Hollytail must be. 'I'm sure we can find them! Ozzy and I have tracked down missing animals before.'

'Let's start by climbing to the treetops. You can spot so much more when you're up high.' Ozzy began clambering up the tree.

'I'll come too.'

Hollytail started climbing the tree trunk but she caught her injured paw on a sharp twig. Yowling, she lost her balance and tumbled to the ground.

'You need to rest your paw.'
Kitty knelt beside her. 'Why don't you
stay here. Then if the kittens come
home, you'll be waiting for them.'

'I could stay with you if you
like?' said Pumpkin. 'It's easy to let
worries fill your head if you're by
yourself.'

Hollytail frowned at Pumpkin
and flicked her tail. 'Well, stay if you
must. As long as my kittens are found
I don't care!'

Pumpkin looked a little
unsure, but Kitty smiled at him
and nodded. She waited for the
two cats to get settled in the
hollow of the tree. Then
she climbed swiftly
after Ozzy.

The wind grew fiercer as Kitty climbed higher. The tree rocked like a boat and the branches creaked. In the distance, there was a rumble of thunder.

Kitty went on climbing, her eyes fixed on the top of the tree. The missing kittens could be almost anywhere in the forest. It would take all their superpowers to find the little cats and bring them safely home again.

Chapter 4

Kitty felt her superpowers tingling through her body as she pulled herself up the tree. Ozzy was waiting at the top, his feathery cloak flapping in the stormy wind.

'The forest is even bigger than

I thought,' he said to Kitty. 'Look—there's our orange tent. Doesn't it look tiny?'

Kitty balanced on the branch and stared down at the forest. 'And there's the lake we swam in too.'

Moonlight poured down onto the patchwork of trees and bushes. A small stream ran through the wood, glittering like a silver thread. The lake where they'd swum that morning lay to the right and to the left was the car park full of tiny toy-like cars.

'It's such a big place to search. So where do we start?' wondered Kitty.

'Maybe we should split up. It'll be much quicker!' suggested Ozzy.

Thunder rumbled again in the distance and Kitty frowned. 'I don't think we should split up. There might be a storm coming.'

'But it'll be faster,' Ozzy insisted.

'We don't know the wood very well so one of us might get lost,' Kitty explained. 'Anyway, our superpowers mean we work better as a team. I can climb and balance the best, but you can swoop through the trees much faster than me! You can see further in the dark, but my super-hearing is stronger.'

'I guess you're right. I can see further than anyone!' Turning his head slowly, Ozzy used his night vision to scan the forest below. 'I thought we'd

spot the kittens easily from up here, but
I can only see mice and voles and deer.'

Kitty strained her eyes and ears,
pouring every bit of her superpowers
into trying to spot the kittens.
Everywhere she looked, little creatures
were moving in the undergrowth. There
were mice squeaking, squirrels rustling,
and foxes padding through the trees,
but no sign of the little cats.

Olive swooped down from the
moonlit sky and landed beside them
with a soft swish of her wings. She
fluffed her snowy-white feathers.
Ozzy! Kitty!' she hooted. 'Is something
wrong? I went to stretch my wings
and when I came back to the tent
you'd gone.'

Ozzy explained about the wildcat's missing kittens. 'We need to find them fast! Can you help us?'

Olive nodded. 'Of course! But it won't be easy. This forest is full of secret places—tiny caves and hollows and bramble patches.'

'Hollytail told us the kittens loved playing by the stream. I think we should start there,' said Kitty.

'There's no point going to the stream,' said Ozzy, frowning. 'She said she'd looked there already.'

'I know! But it gives us a place to
start.' Kitty ran along the branch
and jumped to the next
tree, and Ozzy spread
his cloak and flew
after her.

The wind grew stronger as Kitty
and Ozzy darted through the treetops.
Ozzy glided along with his cloak
stretched wide, while Kitty leapt and
somersaulted from branch to branch.
Lightning flashed in the distance and

dark rainclouds moved closer.

At last, Kitty swung down to the
ground and landed on the narrow
riverbank. Ozzy flew smoothly to the
earth, and Olive swooped down and
settled on his shoulder.

The stream poured over a jumble of rocks and pebbles. Ferns grew along the bank, stretching their leaves to touch the glittering, moonlit water.

'There's no sign of the kittens here.' Ozzy folded his arms. 'I think we should go back to the treetops. We can search the wood quicker from up there.'

'Wait a minute!' Kitty spotted a row of stones that led across the

stream. 'Those are the stepping stones that Hollytail was talking about.' Rushing over, she jumped on to the first stone and used them to skip across the water. She imagined the three little kittens doing exactly the same.

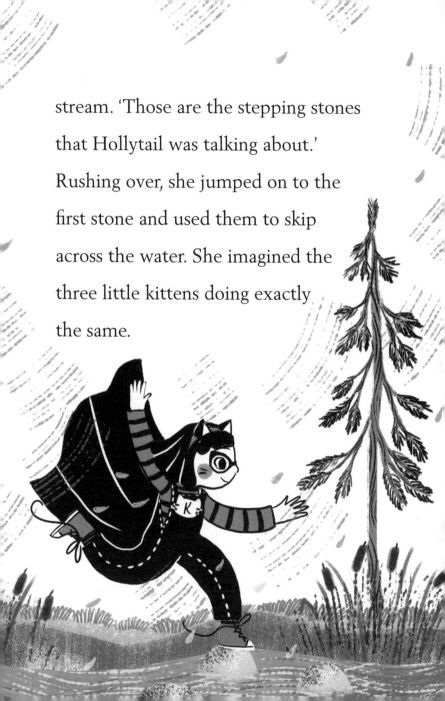

'Look at those trampled ferns. That could've been the kittens.' Olive nodded to the squashed leaves.

'And look at this!' Kitty pulled a wisp of grey fur off a bramble.

'That might be fox's fur or a squirrel's,' Ozzy told her.

'But these pawprints are definitely a kitten's!' Kitty pointed triumphantly at the line of pawprints in the soft mud beside the riverbank. 'Now we just have to follow the trail.'

They tried to follow the pawprints

but the trail led round and round in circles, before ending at the water's edge.

A vole darted out of the bushes, stopping to look at Kitty and Ozzy in surprise.

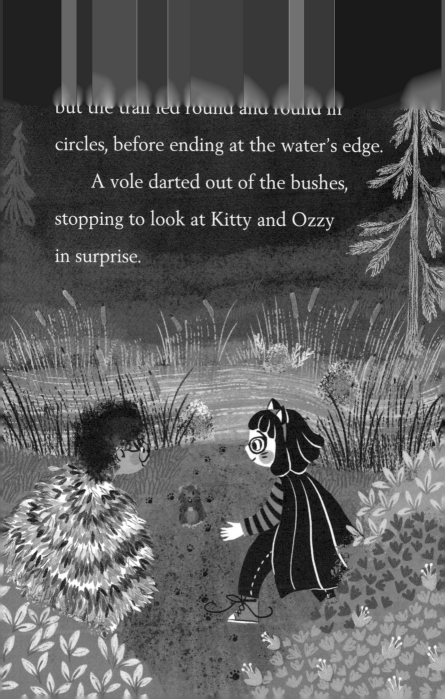

'Hello! We're looking for some lost kittens,' said Kitty. 'Have you seen them?'

The vole shook his head. 'There was a full-grown cat here this morning. She yowled at me and I ran away!' He looked around fearfully. 'I hope she's not coming back. She looked scary!'

He darted back into the bushes again.

Kitty rubbed her forehead. Surely the pawprints must lead somewhere! But no matter how hard she looked, she couldn't find a proper trail. The pawprints only led to the water.

Ozzy frowned deeply. 'You don't think they fell in the stream, do you? They probably can't swim!'

Kitty's stomach turned over. If the kittens had been playing here, they might easily have fallen in. 'The water's really shallow, so they wouldn't be in any danger.

But maybe they slid downstream and that's why we can't find a pawprint trail.'

Olive launched into the air, her snowy wings spread wide. 'Then let's follow the stream. Maybe they're not as far away as we thought.'

Kitty's heart raced as she ran along the riverbank. If the kittens had fallen in the water they would be cold and wet and scared. Speeding up, she

followed the twisting stream as it
tumbled over a little waterfall.
The rainclouds drew closer,
blocking out the moon.
The wind rocked the trees
and rain began to fall.

'Kitty, wait a second!' Ozzy called over the howling wind. 'The kittens could be hiding from the storm. Maybe we should carry on searching in the morning.'

'But what if they're frightened?' cried Kitty. 'And they could be quite close by! Let's look for a bit longer.'

'But you don't even know if you're going the right way!' said Ozzy.

Kitty leapt over the waterfall.
Then she raced down the hill, stopping
suddenly at the bottom.

The lake lay in front of her, rippling
in the wind. There was no sign of the
kittens—no pawprints on the shore or
tufts of grey fur on the bushes.

Olive circled around the lake and then flew back to Kitty. 'I can't see them anywhere, I'm afraid.'

'I told you!' Ozzy caught up with them, panting. 'We were probably going the wrong way all the time.'

Lightning flashed right above the trees. Kitty wiped the rain off her face and her heart sank. The kittens were still lost somewhere and she was as far away from finding them as ever.

Chapter 5

Rain drummed on the surface of the lake. Kitty and Ozzy dived under a tree to find shelter. Lightning flashed again followed by a roll of thunder that made the ground tremble. Kitty's heart raced and she steadied herself against the trunk of the tree.

'Maybe we should get back to the
campsite. I'm soaking!' Ozzy shook the
rain off his cloak.

'But the kittens need us! We have
to keep going.' Kitty ran to the water's

edge and stared across the lake. Surely there was a clue somewhere that pointed to where the kittens had gone.

There was another flash of lightning. Kitty took a deep breath and focused on using her super senses. Her night vision let her see through the dark and her super-hearing picked up every tiny sound. Beneath the noise of the wind and rain, there was a faint mewing.

'I can hear something!' Kitty followed the sound along the water's edge and Ozzy dashed after her.

The mewing
stopped suddenly and Kitty
stared around. 'Did you
hear that noise? Where
was it coming from?'

'I heard it!' Ozzy
began climbing the nearest
tree. 'I'll look around from
up here.'

Kitty crept forwards, listening carefully. The rain began to slow and the next flash of lightning was further away in the distance. Rainwater dripped from every leaf and branch. Kitty took a deep breath, drinking in the smell of earth and leaves. Then she caught the scent of cats.

Leaping forwards, she tracked the scent through the trees. Dodging around brambles and jumping over logs, she raced through the forest.

'Keep going!' Ozzy called down.

'I can see them at the top of a tree.'

The mewing grew louder and louder.

'Is anyone there?' a kitten called squeakily.

'Help me—I'm going to fall!' cried another.

Kitty ran faster, her feet drumming on the ground. A mouse ran out of its hole to watch her and a squirrel family peered out of their nest. Up ahead, she spotted a big oak tree with three little animals clinging to the top.

Swinging from branch to branch, she reached the tree just as the moon came out from behind the clouds. Silvery moonlight poured down through the leaves. Balanced on the end of the topmost branch were three rain-soaked kittens. They stared down at Kitty. Their damp fur was smeared with earth and leaves.

'Kittens! Are you all right?' cried Kitty.

The little cats peered down at her with big round eyes. The wind rocked the oak tree. The kitten's branch gave a loud crack and Kitty gasped.

Gliding down from a nearby tree, Ozzy landed beside her. 'Their branch is broken. It must have snapped in the storm.'

'Help us!' cried the largest kitten. 'We're stuck up here.'

'I just want to go home!' wailed a second kitten.

The smallest kitten mewed sadly
as she scrambled along the wet branch.
Her paws slipped and she almost fell.
Squealing, she clung to the branch with
one claw.

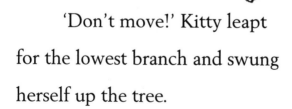

'Don't move!' Kitty leapt
for the lowest branch and swung
herself up the tree.

Climbing as fast as she could, she reached the top of the tree in a few seconds. Somersaulting through the air, she caught hold of the dangling kitten and landed neatly on the branch below. Passing the first kitten down to Ozzy, she climbed up to rescue the others.

'Are you OK?' she asked them breathlessly.

'My stomach's all growly and I miss my mummy!' said the first kitten.

'Me too!' the other kitten sobbed.

Kitty gathered them into her arms and sprang gracefully down the tree.

Setting them down on the ground, she crouched beside them. 'I'm Kitty and this is Ozzy, and we're superheroes-in-training. We've been searching for you all night.'

'I'm Briar,' said the largest kitten, 'and this is Hazelnut and Little-leaf.' He pointed to the cat with dark-brown fur and the smallest kitten.

'You know you shouldn't have wandered off without telling anyone,' Kitty began.

'We're really sorry!' mewed Briar.

'We were looking for our mummy and we got a bit lost. So we climbed up this tree to see if we could find her—'

'But it was too high and we couldn't get down again,' added Hazelnut.

'We must have been up there for WEEKS AND WEEKS!' cried Little-leaf.

'At least you're safe now!'
Kitty said, scooping up Briar and
Hazelnut. 'Let's get you back home.'

Ozzy picked up Little-leaf. The
kitten clambered over his shoulders
and played with the feathers that lined
his cloak.

Kitty made sure Briar and
Hazelnut were holding tight to her
shoulders. Then she swung and leapt
from one tree to the next. Ozzy flew
after her, his cloak fluttering in the
wind. Olive swooped over the treetops

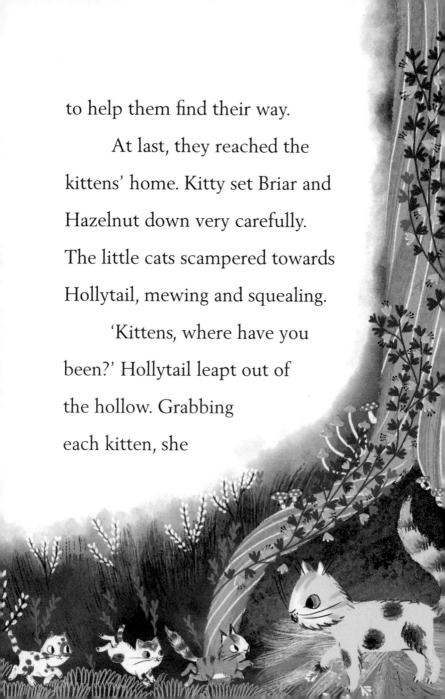

to help them find their way.

At last, they reached the kittens' home. Kitty set Briar and Hazelnut down very carefully. The little cats scampered towards Hollytail, mewing and squealing.

'Kittens, where have you been?' Hollytail leapt out of the hollow. Grabbing each kitten, she checked them over from head to toe.

'You're back!' said Pumpkin, jumping around in delight. 'Where did you find the kittens?'

'They were a long way from here,' said Kitty, explaining how they'd got stuck in the oak tree.

'I told you NOT to set a paw out of our den—naughty kittens!' Hollytail scolded, but when she thought Kitty wasn't looking she gently groomed their ears and whiskers.

'It's all right, mummy! Kitty and Ozzy brought us home safely,' squeaked Briar.

'Thank you, Kitty!' mewed Hazelnut.

'Thanks, Ozzy!' cried Little-leaf.

Hollytail's eyes narrowed as she looked at Kitty and Ozzy. Then her face twitched into a smile. 'You were lucky, my kittens! Lots of humans are messy and silly. Not many are as wild and brave as these two.'

Chapter

6

'It's time to go to sleep!'
Hollytail told the kittens. 'Come here,
Briar, and you too, Little-leaf. You
should be curled up in bed.'

'But Mummy, we're hungry!'
mewed Little-leaf. 'Can't we have

something to eat?'

'My tummy is really rumbling!'
Hazelnut said, licking her whiskers.

'All right then,' said Hollytail.
'Stay here with Kitty while
I catch some fish.' And
she padded down to
the stream, appearing
a few minutes later
with some fresh fish
to eat.

Kitty found
half a packet of

marshmallows in her pocket so she shared them with Ozzy and they sat down together with the kittens to have a midnight feast. Olive settled on a nearby branch and folded her snowy wings.

'Can you hear that?' said Ozzy suddenly. 'It sounds as if the whole forest is moving.'

Kitty listened. The ground trembled beneath a hundred little footsteps.

There was the tiny patter of mouse feet and the soft pad of a fox. The hollow thud of deer hooves rang out over the flutter of owl wings. Each sound grew closer and closer and closer.

Pumpkin leapt into Kitty's arms, his eyes wide. Hollytail pricked up her ears and flexed her claws.

The beech tree at the edge of the clearing creaked and swayed. Then its branches parted and dozens of animals poured into the clearing. A fox stepped in first followed by a family of mice.

Two crows landed in the branches and a squirrel ran down the tree trunk. A magpie perched beside the squirrel and folded his black-and-white wings. Two voles poked their whiskery faces out of a pile of leaves.

'What's this?' Hollytail drew back in alarm. 'Why are you all here?'

'We came to see them.' A mouse nodded to Kitty and Ozzy, his whiskers trembling.

The wildcat frowned. 'Why? I don't understand.'

'We wanted to meet the superheroes from the city who help animals,' the mouse replied. 'An owl told the fox how they rescued the kittens. Then the fox told the squirrels, and the squirrels told the rabbits, and the rabbits told the voles, and—'

'And the news spread right through

the forest,' interrupted a squirrel. 'We heard you might be having a midnight feast too, so we brought some food with us.' She held out a large acorn. 'Is it all right if we join in?'

'Of course you can!' said Kitty. 'It's really nice to make some new friends.'

'Without the city clocktower we don't know whether it's actually midnight,' Pumpkin pointed out.

'It feels quite late,' said Kitty, yawning. 'I can hardly keep my eyes open. I thought camping in the forest would be quiet and peaceful. I never expected so much action and adventure!'

'It's a good thing you were here to rescue these kittens,' said the squirrel.

'Kitty was amazing!' squeaked Little-leaf. 'She did a somersault right at the top of the tree.'

'Was it scary searching the wood in the storm?' the mouse asked Kitty.

'A little bit, but I knew we had to keep on looking. I was sure we'd find the kittens as long as we didn't give up,' said Kitty, letting the mouse have a nibble of her marshmallow.

Hollytail nodded to Kitty and drew her kittens closer. Briar snuggled down and closed his eyes, and Hazelnut began to purr.

'I think this has been one of my favourite adventures,' Kitty added.

'Mine too!' Ozzy agreed. 'I love the city but I really like the forest too.'

'It just shows that it doesn't matter where you are,' Pumpkin said sleepily as he curled up on Kitty's lap. 'As long as you're with your friends.'

Super Facts
About Cats

Super Speed

Have you ever seen a cat make a quick escape
from a dog? If so, you'll know that they can move
really fast—up to 30mph!

Super Hearing

Cats have an incredible sense of hearing
and can swivel their large ears to pinpoint
even the tiniest of sounds.

Super Reflexes

Have you ever heard the saying 'cats always
land on their feet'? People say this because
cats have amazing reflexes. If a cat is falling,
they can sense quickly how to move their
bodies into the right position to land safely.

Super Leaps

A cat can jump over eight feet high
in a single leap; this is due to its powerful
back leg muscles.

Super Vision

Cats have amazing night-time vision. Their
incredible ability to see in low light allows them
to hunt for prey when it's dark outside.

Super Smell

Cats have a very powerful sense of smell,
14 times stronger than a human's. Did you know
that the pattern of ridges on each cat's nose
is as unique as a human's fingerprint?

About the author

Paula Harrison

Before launching a successful writing career,
Paula was a Primary school teacher. Her years teaching
taught her what children like in stories and how
they respond to humour and suspense. She went on
to put her experience to good use, writing many
successful stories for young readers.

About the illustrator

Jenny Løvlie

Jenny is a Norwegian illustrator, designer, creative, foodie, and bird enthusiast. She is fascinated by the strong bond between humans and animals and loves using bold colours and shapes in her work.

Love Kitty?
Why not try these too . . .